HENRY
the Hedgehog

by Anne-Marie Dalmais
Illustrated by Annie Bonhomme

English translation
by Diane Cohen

DERRYDALE BOOKS
New York

Henry has been invited, with his beloved stuffed hedgehog, to his grandparents' house in the mountains.

Grandma has baked a big, glazed apple pie for him.

Sleeping in this huge bed is quite
an adventure! (Henry needs a
small stool to reach the mattress!)
There's nothing like sleeping
under this cozy comforter. It has
so many brightly colored squares
you can't even count them all.

Cuckoo! Cuckoo! The wooden birds sings nine times. Hop! Hop! The little hedgehog springs out of bed, slips on his clothes, and goes down into the garden. There, to his surprise, he discovers a vegetable patch surrounded by a row of raspberry bushes.

After he has tasted a handful of
these fragrant little fruits, Henry
finds his grandfather near the
woodpile. "Here's a nice, sturdy
log." Grandpa says. "It's just what
we need to make you a swing."

With two heavy pieces of rope,

they hang the small board from

the branches of a pine tree.

"Higher! Higher!" cries Henry,

thrilled at being way up in the air.

"I want to go as high as this big

tree!"

At night, by the fire, Grandma Hedgehog reads a story. Grandpa Hedgehog builds a little wooden armchair for Henry, and Henry, who likes to play "handyman," helps as best he can. Oh, what a lovely evening they are having!

The next morning, it rains very
hard.

"Not to worry," assures Grandma
Hedgehog. "We'll spend some time
looking around in the attic."

To get there, they fearlessly climb
a very steep ladder.

What treasures they find upstairs!

It's a magical place where Henry

discovers, to his delight, wonderful

old-fashioned toys.

He learns how to spin tops and

spends the whole morning playing

with them.

Today, the Hedgehogs are going to

have lunch with their neighbors,

the Woodchucks.

Henry has never seen a house

quite like this one. It's a mound of

grass with a pretty, wooden door.

And there isn't one single window!

Grandpa rings the bell.

Next, Henry enters their cozy, underground home, complete with many passageways, perfect for playing hide-and-seek! He immediately becomes friends with the three Woodchuck children! Henry is very happy. He didn't expect his vacation to be filled with so many wonderful surprises!